Peeping Beauty

By
Brenda Maier

Illustrated by
Zoe Waring

Aladdin

NEW YORK   LONDON   TORONTO   SYDNEY   NEW DELHI

To James, for our
happily ever after —B. M.

For my special mama hen, with love —Z. W.

🪔 ALADDIN / An imprint of Simon & Schuster Children's Publishing Division / 1230 Avenue of the Americas, New York, New York 10020 / First Aladdin hardcover edition February 2019 / Text copyright © 2019 by Brenda Maier / Illustrations copyright © 2019 by Zoe Waring / All rights reserved, including the right of reproduction in whole or in part in any form. / ALADDIN and related logo are registered trademarks of Simon & Schuster, Inc. / For information about special discounts for bulk purchases, please contact Simon & Schuster Special Sales at 1-866-506-1949 or business@simonandschuster.com. / The Simon & Schuster Speakers Bureau can bring authors to your live event. For more information or to book an event contact the Simon & Schuster Speakers Bureau at 1-866-248-3049 or visit our website at www.simonspeakers.com. / Book designed by Karin Paprocki / The illustrations for this book were rendered digitally. / The text of this book was set in Cabin Sketch. / Manufactured in China 1118 SCP / 2 4 6 8 10 9 7 5 3 1 / Library of Congress Cataloging-in-Publication Data | Names: Maier, Brenda, author. | Waring, Zoe, illustrator. | Title: Peeping Beauty | by Brenda Maier ; illustrated by Zoe Waring. | Description: First Aladdin hardcover edition. | New York : Aladdin, 2019. | Summary: As a family of chickens waits for the final egg to hatch, Mama reads favorite fairy tales. | Identifiers: LCCN 2017007911 (print) | LCCN 2017034269 (eBook) | ISBN 9781481472739 (eBook) | ISBN 9781481472722 (hc) | Subjects: | CYAC: Eggs–Fiction. | Chickens–Fiction. | Books and reading–Fiction. | Classification: LCC PZ7.1.M3468 (eBook) | LCC PZ7.1.M3468 Pee 2019 (print) | DDC [E]–dc23 | LC record available at https://lccn.loc.gov/2017007911

nce upon a time, on a faraway farm, Mama and Papa read to their eggs, nestled them into bed, and kissed them good night.

"This is so egg-citing! By tomorrow we'll have three little ones."

Just as the sun rose . . .

QUIVER
SHIVER
CRACKLE
PEEP!

No sooner had Mama spoken than . . .

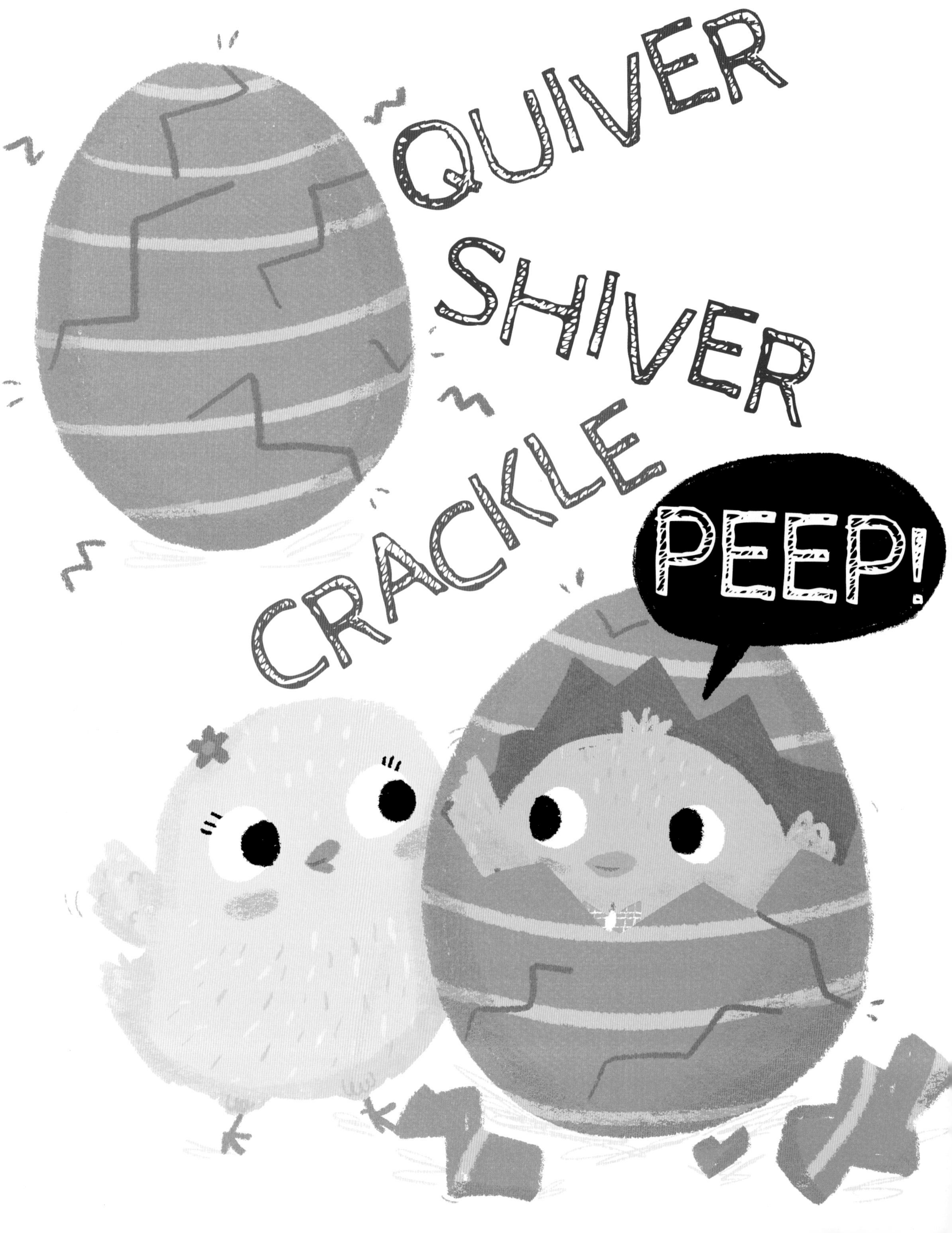
QUIVER
SHIVER
CRACKLE
PEEP!

No sooner had Mama spoken than . . .

The little family flocked around
the third egg and waited.

And waited.

Big sister hatched a plan.

With a cluck-cluck here,
and a cluck-cluck there...

But nothing happened.

Big brother hatched a plan too.

Still nothing happened.

Maybe we just need to be patient.

Mama read *The Princess and the Peacock*. The first little chick closed her eyes.

Mama read *Beauty and the Beak*. The second little chick closed his eyes.

Then Mama began her favorite story, *Peeping Beauty*. Even Papa closed his eyes.

As Mama read about the princess who wouldn't wake up, she heard a faint sound.

PEEP!

So Mama clucked ahead.

And the rooster gave Peeping Beauty a peck on the cheek . . .

Mama stared at the egg. "Hmmm . . .
I wonder if I should just give it a little extra
love?" The chicks were way ahead of her.

But just then . . .

Another chick scrambled out.

"Oh, for the love of feathers! Twins!"

Mama took attendance one more time, just to be sure.
Then the little chicks cozied up close, fell fast asleep, and
dreamed of all the stories to come.

But our story is going to be the very best story of all.